# Feng NASTY Shui

# Feng NASTY Shui

## Lottie Anderson

COLLINS & BROWN
www.chrysalisbooks.co.uk

First Published in Great Britain in 2005 by
Collins & Brown Limited
Bramley Road
London W10 6SP

An imprint of **Chrysalis** Books Group plc

Distributed in the United States and Canada by Sterling Publishing Co.,
387 Park Avenue
South, New York, NY 10016, USA

British Library Cataloguing-inPublication Data:
A catalogue record for this book is available from the British Library

ISBN: 1 84340 314 5

Editor: Victoria Alers-Hankey
Design: e-Digital Design
Illustrations: Gareth Hobbs for e-Digital Design

Reproduction by Classicscan Ltd, Singapore
Printed at Kyodo Printing Ltd, Singapore

# Contents

'The five elements and
yin and yang energies
balance perfectly.'

# Introduction

*Feng shui, the ancient art of rejigging a room to improve your wealth, health and happiness, is more popular now than, well, since it was first 'invented' more than 4,000 years ago in rural China. It works by creating a harmonious relationship between humans and their environment: living spaces are arranged so that the five elements (earth, water, wood, metal and fire) and yin and yang energies balance perfectly. Anything that hinders the favourable flow of energy, or chi, must be removed, and sharp edges swiftly eliminated to negate sha chi (bad chi). The result of all this reshuffling is years of good luck and bountiful fortune.*

**'Why not look after number one?'**

As you might expect with such easy-access orientalism, feng shui has its fair share of celebrity devotees. Boy George and Sting and Donald Trump are just two of the rich and famous who have had their mansions feng shui-ed, while David Beckham has mystical symbols sewn inside his soccer boots. Less obvious followers include Prince Charles, who invited a feng shui consultant to Highgrove (he had probably heard how inauspicious Buckingham Palace is with The Mall pointing menacingly at its front gates), and the British prime minister Tony Blair, who once employed a feng shui master to re-energize his workspace.

All these people, no doubt, employed feng shui for the most virtuous of purposes. However, feng shui can also be put to much more devious uses. Its strict rules are ripe for messing with, for flipping upside down and bending to suit your own needs. A cunning twist of the basic theories, such as placing a mirror in an unlucky corner of your ex's bedroom, will cause endless amounts of mischief – not to say a distinct lack of post-ex sex. You could also opt for a dose of duplicity: giving a plant to a new work colleague, someone who is secretly after your job, may seem like a thoughtful gesture, but not if the plant is a cactus with spikes that produce damaging, negative chi. Oops! Best of all, though, who would think to blame you, especially since you've been so generous.

Nasty feng shui is feng shui that works for you. It's machiavellian, to be sure, but why not look after number one? After all, since good feng shui is all about engineering your own good luck and controlling your life, why not use it to cunningly control the lives of others? The results could get you the partner of your dreams, a massive pay rise, turn your former nemesis into your slave – essentially, make you king or queen of the world. Really, what could be better?

'Love is all down to
destiny? Pur-lease.'

## Chapter One
# Love and Hate

*You really think love is all down to destiny? Pur-lease. If you believe that, you're probably still single or, even worse, stuck in a going-nowhere relationship. Love – or rather lust, which could eventually lead to love – is all about seduction, about plotting and persuasion, about charming your way into your prey's affections and oh-so-subtle mind control. The same strategy goes for love's sister emotion: hate. With some naughty feng shui tricks, you can direct your passions with precision planning and manipulate nature to suit your own needs. Did you know, for instance, that by turning your bed around to face a certain direction, you can improve your sex life? Or that a cute pair of mandarin duck statuettes in the correct corner of your house should result in swiftly entrapping the man or woman of your dreams? And how about getting revenge on your ex by instantly lowering their libido – and tempting their new partner to stray? When it comes to affairs of the heart, nasty feng shui is Dangerous Liaisons-style game playing with an oriental edge. Whether your aim is to get a ring on your finger – or metaphorically wring the neck of your lying, cheating ex – read on.*

# Why am I always single?

*If you are one of those people who is lucky in life but unlucky in love, you can turn your love luck around with some clever feng shui. When you look out of your bedroom window, what do you see? Lots of right angles? Sharp corners of buildings, for example, or the corners of roofs or even church spires all pointing towards your bed? Thought so: these are known as secret, or poison, arrows, and they are directing sha chi, or bad chi, straight into your love life – or rather lack of it. This is why you are always alone – after all, who would want to find themselves in such an inauspicious place as your bed? Rectify this immediately: buy lots of mirrors and strategically place them to reflect the sha chi back out of your bedroom. Soon you will be the target of the right kind of arrow – namely, cupid's.*

## How to force anyone – and everyone – to fall for you

'Feng shui isn't magic!' cry all the experienced and ever-so-earnest practitioners, but let's face it, sometimes it feels like it is. This is particularly the case when it comes to love, when a simple 'spell' can help one become two. Acclaimed masters recommend that the perennially single place a bowl of water on their windowsill along the east-west axis of their home, ideally in a spot that catches the afternoon sun. Every morning when the singleton wakes up, the bowl must be replenished with fresh water. Sooner or later, it will be raining new lovers.

**'Sooner or later it will be raining new lovers.'**

## Pander to their passion personality

Anyone who has studied even the most basic of psychology (think the agony column in your average women's magazine) will know that to get things going, you need to pander to the object of your affection's personality. At the same time, you need to remain sufficiently self-aware to step up or tone down certain aspects of your own character that might complement – or clash – with his or hers, simultaneously while anticipating and adapting to their fluctuating moods. It's tricky stuff.

A similar principle works in feng shui, which purports that people are either yin or yang. You are probably already familiar with the yin-yang symbol: intertwining black and white half-circles, each containing a dot of the corresponding colour. The idea is not that the world is comprised of opposing forces, but rather that each force is mutually dependent because neither can exist without the other.

Enough of the science: did you realize that by deducing your potential prey's yin-yang personality, you could further plot your strategy to charm your way into their heart – or their pants? Thought that would regain your attention.

## A yin personality

Yin means 'the moon' and is associated with the feminine side of life. Yin people tend to be passive, easygoing and reflective, but extremely

receptive and open to new ideas. Naturally yin people will have an oval-shaped face, large eyes and a thin frame.

- Seduce them with ... your flexible yoga moves.
- Suggest for supper ... a too-good-to-be-true melange of salad and fruit, finished off with ice cream, a surprisingly yin food.
- Dress yin with ... slouchy, casual clothes and crafty, artesian jewellery.
- Shock their system with ... an invitation to go kick boxing – working out their aggression could do them the world of good.

## A yang personality

Yang means 'the sun' and is linked to the more masculine side of life. Yang people are active and spontaneous. They are ambitious, decisive and a force to be reckoned with. You can spot a natural-born yang person a mile off: a round face, short, stocky frame and small eyes. Lovely. Of course, they cannot be yang all the time – they would simply explode.

- Seduce them with ... your super-logical mind and ability to play chess like a grand master.
- Suggest for supper ... fish, meat and eggs. And for pudding? A heart attack.
- Dress yang with ... bright colours and structured styles. A true yang would be totally over-wowed by a scarlet suit.
- Shock their system with ... a great massage. Yangs need to chill out – and need all the help they can get.

# How to make any man your slave

*Feng shui can play a part in getting the object of your affection to notice you, and all by a subtle rearrangement of your house. First, you need to get your bearings – quite literally – so invest in a compass to find out where everything sits in your home. Is the bathroom to the north? Your bedroom to the south? It all counts.*

The best position for a bedroom – and thus your love prospects – is in the south-east corner, the direction that symbolizes romance. Enhance your luck with some clever decoration – lush plants, crystals and water features all attract love. If you are looking for something long-term and in writing (ie, marriage), you should buy some peonies. In China, the peony symbolizes marriage – a family home full of peonies indicates that the household includes eligible daughters of marrying age, for instance – and placing these flowers in the south-west corner of your bedroom will increase your chances of a proposal. If you don't fancy a twice-weekly trip to the florist (dead or dying flowers are extremely inauspicious), a painting will do.

The walls, if you're clever, should be painted a soft yellow – this is the colour most associated with fruitful relationships. Your bed should have its pillows pointing towards the west, so spin them around. For a total assault on the senses, whip out an oil burner and start wafting soothing vanilla scents through your home – this fragrance is considered

**'Whip out an oil burner and start wafting vanilla scents.'**

best for attracting men. Wear it as a perfume, too. With any luck, they will be following you Pied Piper-style in no time.

## A brief lesson in what a man wants

Men want a siren. They want someone sexily brazen, someone who will make the first move, be dominant but not clingy, self-confident with an air of mystery. Simple, yes? Er, no, which is why you should start polishing those crystals pronto.

Crystals are perfect for attracting a man into your life – and so pretty, as well! Natural crystals or a chandelier in the south-west and south-east corners will bring in the boys, especially if the crystals are placed to attract maximum sunlight – all those prisms floating around will instantly maximize your boyfriend potential. You should hang them from red ribbons, another lucky talisman.

If the sound of gentle tinkling in the wind doesn't annoy you too much, add some wind chimes to your boudoir's south-west corner. However, make sure they are made of wood and are hollow so the chi can flow freely.

## Drop-dead passion fashion

The right sartorial shui is crucial if you want to ensnare that man, so when mulling over what to wear to catch that gorgeous boy's attention, plan carefully. As any fashionista knows, accessories are key to pulling a look together. Red and pink silk ribbons are deemed a feng shui man-magnet, so start channelling that sexy schoolgirl look now. A less full-on option is to tie a red ribbon to your handbag. Super-long talons, preferably painted red or pink, will also make you irresistible to men.

'Super-long talons make you irresistible.'

As for footwear, red shoes are perfect because red is the best colour to get energy – and therefore passion – fired up, although you should avoid shoes that are too pointy since the sharp toes act as daggers, metaphorically cutting through the chi and poisoning any chance of romance. Likewise, save those Eighties-inspired thunderbolt earrings for clubbing because jewellery with jagged edges acts as poisonous arrows. Also leave any abstract prints at home. Anything geometric and just a little bit wacky confuses the chi and thus bounces back those love vibes your date might be attempting to send.

## Lust-inducing lingerie

Think oh-so-raunchy red. If red seems too racy – and, let's face it, too Vegas – plump for pink. Both colours, especially in silk, are guaranteed to spice up your love life. If it's more than a passing fling, however, opt for green. This seemingly unsexy colour is perfect for long-lasting commitments – if he doesn't freak out at the sight of Kermit-coloured lace, you must be on to a winner.

## Make your house less of a spinster's lair

The traditional signs of spinsterhood in the West – namely, an abundance of cushions on the sofa and a love of cats – is not deemed bad in feng shui terms. What is bad, though, is too much frou-frou decor. This means lots of lace, satin, silk and general pinkness – it's all too yin. Balance this with more yang – think leather furniture and dark, more masculine, colours.

Singletons should also rid their homes of any images of single women – not only the ones of you on holiday, but also paintings and artwork of girls on their own. Replace these with pictures of couples, the more in love the better. Well, that is what you want, isn't it?

### Sneaky strategies for a first date

Once your plotting, planning and purchases of crystals have paid off and you have snagged that first date, don't get complacent – you want to keep him interested. If your date is in a restaurant, you are in luck – that way you can dictate the events of the evening. More than soft lighting or foods with aphrodisiac qualities, it is where you sit that counts. Make sure your man is facing west. This is the ideal direction for romance – he'll be smitten the second he takes his seat – or better still, sit side by side. If you are both facing west, then oh, what's that? The distant sound of wedding bells?

### Seduce him into staying interested

After all that effort, the last thing you want is for the object of your affection to stray. Luckily, feng shui comes in useful here, too.

Start mixing your things together to bring both of your energies closer. This is a big step and famously one that freaks out many men – think

how quickly they will run at the first sight of your toothbrush in their bathroom cabinet – so do it gradually. You could start with your shoes:

**'Men run at the first sign of a toothbrush.'**

mix them up with his by the front door or bed or wherever he leaves them. Then move on to your coats and start leaving yours on top of his. Continue mixing until you don't know where he ends and you begin. Sigh.

## Put on the red light

Sometimes, just to up the ante on your sex appeal, you need to make like Roxanne and put on the red light. Quite literally. A red light or lantern in the south-west corner of your house – or, better still, your bedroom – is the best way to lure a man in there. Try to keep it subtle, though – if it looks too pervy, you won't see your lover for dust.

## How to get that ring on your finger

So you think he's going to pop the question. You've seen him lingering in front of jewellers' shops, phoning romantic restaurants, looking cutely anxious ... but you don't want him to lose his nerve. Give him some encouragement, then, using your clothes. Nasty Feng Shui dictates that tiered clothing gets in the way of commitments, so even if layering is en vogue, stick with one stream-lined item – namely, a dress. Colour counts, too: red and pink, shades that universally represent love, are perfect. Blue, on the other hand, might make you appear too remote and ice maidenly. Another sign to motivate him is a red rose placed in the south-west corner of your house. Just make sure he realizes that it's not from another admirer.

## Make sure you have a mummy's boy

Every mother secretly wants a little boy, someone who'll see their mum as the unattainable perfection of womenhood in later life. You're not asking much! After marriage comes children, and feng shui can help here, too. For once, the onus on conception is with the father. According to Chinese tradition, a couple's fertility luck is all down to him and his ancestors – so you had better keep them happy. One way is to make sure that your man is sufficiently reverential to the north-west position, the direction that symbolizes his ancestors' luck. Make sure he sleeps, eats and even works facing that way. For added luck, place an electric fan in the north-west corner of the bedroom, and keep it on all night to churn the chi continually. A couple should also remember what, exactly, a bedroom is for and remove any excess paraphernalia – TVs, computer and so on – so they can concentrate their efforts.

In this newly serene and near-empty space, add some tasteful ornaments. Feng shui is big on animals as symbols, and elephants represent pregnancy. Place a pair on either side of the door. And if you secretly want a boy, make sure the elephants are big and showy.

# How to make any woman fall for your charms

*A cunning chap can easily feng shui himself into being the ultimate seducer. According to Chinese lore, romance, luck and marriage luck work in the same way for men, since ancient culture allowed a man to have several wives and concubines. According to the same ancient tradition, good marriage luck for women, on the other hand, was to be happy first wives – and then subsequently well looked after if a younger model came along. Hmmmm, not so good, then.*

Times have changed but feng shui has not, so if a man adheres to the following rules, he should get love and marriage – and, unlike women, will never have to worry about his partner's roving eye.

## Sort out your bathroom habits

This goes for girls as well. If your bathroom or anywhere with a basin or sink lies in the south-west corner of your house, you are in trouble. The south-west sector symbolizes love and marriage, and the continual turbulence of the water will affect your love life. In other words, every time you flush the toilet or remove the basin plug, you are quite literally flushing away your relationship. You are also ruining any chance of even having a relationship if you're still single.

**'You are flushing away your relationship.'**

If possible, stop using that particular toilet or sink. If that's not an option, leave the plug in when the basin isn't in use and always keep the toilet lid down. Add more metal chi energy to the decor – think metal towel rails, stone flooring and the colour grey. Forget about adding any warming knick-knacks and don't even think about using a crystal – for once, this will only make matters worse. Better still, hide the toilet from view – put it behind curtains, for instance, and pretend it isn't there. Prudery sometimes pays off.

## Brainwash her with your feminine side

Just as a single woman's house should not look too girly, a bachelor pad should have just the right balance of yin and yang. Create harmony by adding a touch of girliness to your home – after all, no woman is going to get turned on by your giant plasma screen TV and alphabeticalized DVD collection. Instead, you need to be just metrosexual enough. A really easy way of doing this is to place some red and pink flowers in a silver-coloured vase and position it at the base of your bed (which should, incidentally, be pointing west). Fresh flowers are best – this will bring you extra merit points from the ladies – but artificial will do as long as you remember to dust them regularly (undusted means bad chi). In addition, hang a small round mirror behind the vase to increase the flower power. Bingo! Your pad has become an instant babe magnet, and none of the girls can quite work out why.

'How to gain points with the ladies.'

### The right flowers to lure her into bed

Flowers always, always work but, if you want your bunch to work a little bit harder, make sure they include the appropriate blooms – the after-thoughts found in cellophane on most garage forecourts just will not do. Instead, plump for peonies, roses, hibiscus or the more exotic lotus flower – all symbolize love, so a sprig or two should work wonders. For real cads hoping for a bit more than a peck on the cheek, give orchids – the scent is an aphrodisiac that, if you play your cards right, could lead to some serious bedroom action. In fact, a pair of orchids placed in the bedroom is particularly auspicious. And although it's not totally feng shui, it might be worth bearing in mind that women also like diamonds and boats …

# Suss out your partner's sexual prowess

*When you have finally made it to their bedroom, stop and look around: with some nifty detective work, the bedroom can instantly reveal how good your new lover will be in bed. Again, it's all down to the way their bed faces. If your lover-to-be sleeps with their head facing north, this is a sure-fire guarantee that they will be an animal between the sheets. Watch out, though, as north is also the best direction for conception, so remember to use birth control.*

A slight inclination to the right, however, and you will be in for a rough night – and not that kind of rough. A bed facing north-east could give you nightmares – no feng shui practitioner ever suggests that anyone should sleep in this direction. If your lover has been doing this, you will know they have a troubled mind. Beware.

## How to become dynamite in bed

Again, some clever crystal hanging can work wonders, this time in the north, the direction associated with sex. Alternatively, place a bowl of quartz crystals in your bedroom: this will usher a powerful yang energy into the room. Hey presto! You will be at it like rabbits – yet another lucky Chinese symbol, in case you were wondering.

**'Hey presto! You'll be at it like rabbits.'**

## Fire up your lagging libido

A low libido could be due to the position of your bathroom – is nowhere good enough, you're probably wondering? A bathroom in the north part of your house can represent a lack of sexual energy. However, it's easily correctable. Simply convert your bathroom into a lush oasis-like environment – add plenty of plants and jungle-green wall colours and you should be back to your former sex god – or goddess – status in no time.

## Make him love you – until the day he dies

For long-term coupling, you must start thinking in twos: two toasters, two tubes of toothpaste (although maybe stop at two beds). Best, though, is a pair of mandarin ducks, which symbolize two people together. This oh-so-tasteful ornament should be placed in the south-west corner of your house – the area, in other words, that best symbolizes conjugal bliss. If you don't fancy ducks, peacocks or even a couple of budgies will do.

On the other hand, when it comes to clothes, think as one. Wearing your lover's wardrobe will bring both of your energies even closer – although if you have got an important business meeting, it might be wise to leave your girlfriend's cocktail dress at home.

A happy relationship should also be free from any game playing. In feng shui, this literally translates to all kinds of games, not only ones played in the mind, so remove any board games from display. Certainly don't stash them in your bedroom. Also clear any clutter from your former favourite storage space – namely, under your bed. Any debris under this important relationship symbol spells disaster.

# How to make sure he never, ever cheats

*You might think that a strategically placed mirror over the bed is the perfect way to spice up your love life but, according to the dictates of feng shui, the polar opposite will happen: he is guaranteed to cheat. Feng shui masters believe that if you create the perfect balance in your house, neither party will feel the urge to stray, and that since a mirror placed in the bedroom doubles the couple's image, this in turn symbolizes an affair. Mirror tiles are worse still – all those tiny fractured images represent multiple cheating.*

## Love rat revenge

Okay, you've ignored all the above and – surprise! – he's cheated. Fear not, though, as feng shui can still be used, this time to wreak

**'Surprise! – he's cheated.'**

your revenge. Now, your mother probably told you that pointing is impolite, but pointing can also bring bad luck, so the next time you spot him, say in a crowded bar or across the street, make sure that you point him out to your friends – then watch his world unravel before your eyes.

## He may have dumped you but now he wants you back

Isn't this the scenario every dumpee dreams of? When the dumper wants you back – but you can gleefully spurn his advances in the knowledge that you have managed to move on? A spot of crafty feng shui can help you with this, too. Somehow you have got to weasel your way into his bedroom. Claim that you have left an earring behind and that he is so slap-dash he will never find it. Then, when his back is turned, stash a picture of yourself in a stagnant chi corner of the room. This will be a corner where the steady flow of chi is blocked – probably one with lots of clutter and superfluous sports equipment (perfect for some sneaky stashing). This lingering image of lust means he will never get you out of his mind – and never quite know why.

## How to take revenge on your ex-lover

Hell hath no fury like someone who has been dumped – and who knows the basics of nasty feng shui. Your former lover has found happiness again while you remain alone and bitter. Not that he knows any of this – instead, badger them for an invitation to their new home and then cause havoc.

Wait for them to leave the room – to make the coffee, for instance. Now you have four minutes to do some simple sabotage. Look for anything that is part of a pair – shoes, candlesticks, whatever. Anything in twos symbolizes a happy couple, so anything divided represents an instant break-up. Kapish?

**'You have four minutes to do some sabotage.'**

## Make him impotent

Ha! The perfect revenge on any man, stripping him of his virility. Impotence is caused by sha chi, so build it up by making his house – or, indeed, his bedroom – into a sha chi target. Aim as many poison arrows – that is, sharp, right-angled objects – at his windows and more specifically his bed. These can include such innocuous objects as a 'For

Sale' sign, so perhaps persuade his neighbours that a sudden housing boom means they should put their home on the market; you, on the other hand, should swivel that sign round the moment it arrives so that its angles are pointing at his windows. Likewise, find a way into his boudoir and rearrange the edges of his furniture or any sharp-edged picture frames towards his bed.

For the grand finale, present him with a cactus. Say it's your let's-stay-friends parting gesture, when in reality it will ensure that he never forgets you in more ways than one. Spiky leaved plants are extremely inauspicious because all those sharp edges are slashing through any positive chi. If possible, place the plant on his bedside table. That'll teach him to mess with you.

### How to take revenge on your ex-lover's new partner

This may sound mean and churlish, but deep down you want him to cheat, don't you? All you have to do is use some nasty feng shui to start his eye roving again: give him – or her – a goldfish. Insist that it is a good will gesture, a sign that you are totally okay. In reality, of course, you are not. A goldfish can be lucky, mainly due to its colour since the

Chinese believe both red and gold to be highly fortuitous. However, a goldfish in the wrong place – on the right side of the front door looking out (claim this is the perfect position so that they never forget to feed their fish) – can cause a great deal of mischief since it attracts the kind of chi that attracts the unattached to the attached. Cue affairs by the dozen – and no one's going to blame Goldie, are they?

'**Keep** your friends close
and your **enemies** closer.'

# Chapter Two
# Friends and Enemies

*To paraphrase Sigmund Freud, no one is happy unless they have friends, and since friends are the 21st-century equivalent of the family, you can never have enough — whatever cunning means you use to cultivate them. One method is to become the consummate party thrower, always serving the perfect food and drink, seating people in the right places and getting the lighting just so. Envious rivals will wonder how you have become such an empress at entertaining; they won't have the first clue that your sneaky strategies are thanks to some nasty feng shui. You can also shower them with gifts — pick the right kind of present and they will start getting tonnes of good luck, subconsciously associating this with you and liking you even more as a result. Give the wrong kind, however, and you will be throwing bad luck in their path. This is where revenge comes in. As any true machiavellian knows, you should keep your friends close and your enemies closer, so start giving sharp items as gifts, sit foes at an awkward corner of a table or wear pointy shoes directed at them. They won't know what's hit them. Better still, they will never know it's you.*

# How to **become** your social set's alpha party thrower

*Transforming yourself into the hostess (or indeed host) with the most-est is the best way to make friends and influence people. Human beings naturally gravitate towards warm homes, good food, stimulating conversation ... and therefore fabulous parties. Becoming a consummate party thrower will therefore give you an enviable position in your group, where you can carve out your own nasty niche.*

This is a position from which you most certainly don't want to be ousted, so before dishing the details on how to give a good party, here is a sneaky secret to ensure you stay ahead of the competition: your party's success is all down to where you, the host, are placed. According to the principles of nasty feng shui, you should make sure that you are always facing the door with your back to the wall. This is by far the most auspicious direction and will ensure that the night goes smoothly. If this is not possible, try to position yourself near a mirror in which the door is reflected, since you want to know who's coming and going. This is the best way to be in control of your party, and to make sure your party-throwing skills will not be usurped.

## Devilish decoration

You know that the best way to make a party swing is to create a seductive atmosphere. An elusive concept, sure, but not if you have a few crafty tricks up your sleeve. First, make sure the overall decor of the room has the yin-yang balance spot on. If your party is in a dining room, paint it in light yet warming tones such as peach or terracotta – this will whet your guests' appetites without overwhelming them. Otherwise they will be too starving – or too stuffed – to relax.

## Manipulate your guests by dressing the perfect table

Alas, the correct decoration does not stop with walls. It continues onto the table. Dressing the perfect table requires lots and lots of shiny, sparkly stuff. Why? Because according to feng shui lore, this will aid the positive flow of chi and thus get your party flowing in no time. So, you had better start polishing the cutlery and high-shining those glasses in preparation. For lots of lively conversation, make sure everything on your table – the linen, the napkins, the lot – comes in shades of blue. Oh, and don't let your dining area be too near the front door – this could play on the minds of your guests and subliminally make them 'inching' to go home.

## Dictate brillant dinner party banter with lighting

Do you really believe that 100-watt strip lighting is going to leave your guests in a super-chilled state? Of course not, which is why candles, whether for a romantic deux à deux or full-on rave, are the perfect solution to lighting. If health and safety is a worry – or you don't trust your friends not to knock over the candelabras – aim for soft-glowing secondary lighting. The shape of the lights is similarly important – nothing should be too angular because all those sharp edges will give off poison arrows, effectively cutting through the positive chi and creating a less-than-harmonious atmosphere. If you are anxious about clever dinner party banter, you must be more specific still. A bunch of blue pendant lights hung low over a dining table should result in the kind of bon mots that would leave Dorothy Parker struggling to keep up.

## A seductive party soundtrack

Since music is supposed to feed the soul and sooth the savage beast, you had better get it right. The dictates of nasty feng shui, somewhat unsurprisingly, state that soothing sounds are imperative for a harmonious atmosphere – think anything involving flutes, bells and that most musical of instruments, wind chimes. Don't overdo it, though, or your party may turn into a meditation session, and don't be tempted to go the other way and play punk – those angry lyrics will only create arguments.

## Other cunning people-attracting party tricks

Still on the subject of assaulting the senses, an oil burner will come in very handy. A burst of the right aromatherapy can instantly clear away any stagnant chi. Tuberose is considered the best scent for parties because it subliminally attracts people to you.

Further boost the yang energy in your home by placing a bowl of lit floating candles, petals, pebbles and small metal pieces in the south-west corner. This combination of elements (earth, fire and water) will attract a positive energy into your house and help get the party in full swing. In no time at all, your guests will be dancing on the tables.

## Seating arrangements for those you dislike

Oh no! Your best friend has invited her irritating know-it-all new boyfriend to your dinner party, and his ranting is bound to dampen everyone else's night. Thankfully, there is a solution. Make sure your table is rectangular and sit him at one of the corners – use place cards to make sure everyone is sitting where you want them. The sharp corners will play havoc with his feng shui and, moreover, his sense of personal comfort. Better still, put him on a corner facing north – this is the relaxation direction, perfect for chilling out but not so good for lively conversation. He will be uncharacteristically quiet all night, leaving the rest of you able to get a word in edgeways.

> 'Oh no! Your best friend has invited her irritating boyfriend.'

You, on the other hand, in your role as uber-host, should always be facing south. This is the most social direction and sitting in this position will instantly transform you into the life and soul of the party.

If you are entertaining a real enemy – say, an ex's new girlfriend or some other such horror – make sure you are wearing a pair of pointy shoes. Sit directly across the table from her and direct your stilettos in her direction. The sharp ends will act as invisible poison arrows and should damage her positive chi,

> 'Damage her positive chi.'

making her seem, well, less attractive. Meanwhile, your ex will have eyes only for you – and he'll have no idea why.

## The ultimate yin-yang party food

Perfectly balanced meals in today's food vocabulary have connotations of health and good diet, and feng shui's 4,000-year-old-plus ideas are no different. Food groups are divided into either yin or yang, and much of what goes together is down to common sense. Yin foods, for instance, include green vegetables, melons and fruit juice, while yang foods are 'heavier' and more substantial – bananas, nuts, fish, meat, spices and chocolate. Try to mix light and heavier foods to create the perfect party food – even if you are simply serving canapés.

## Revenge on a plate

Revenge, of course, is a dish best served cold, so if you're hosting a party and someone on your guest list is an enemy, make sure they always have the 'last' of everything. The last piece of cake, drop of wine – you get the picture. This will create poverty energies, all of which will be directed at him or her, and post-party they will suddenly find themselves on a losing streak.

21cont44344

## And for drinks? Try a feng shui cocktail

Cocktails are the perfect party tipple and a feng shui cocktail will get the balance of both yin and yang flavours spot on. This recipe is courtesy of Ponzu, a pan-Asian restaurant in San Francisco whose decor includes a 125-gallon fish tank – the canny owners obviously know the luck potential of fish!

¾ ounce vodka
¾ ounce gin
¾ ounce rum
¾ ounce triple sec
1½ ounces sweet and sour mix
Splash of lemonade
Splash of blue curaçao

Fill a tall glass with ice. Combine all the ingredients except the curaçao in a shaker of ice. Shake well and strain over the glass. Drizzle the blue curaçao over the top. Enjoy!

## Getting rid of stragglers

There is always one person who refuses to leave, who outstays their welcome and is clueless to boot, so give him the boot by whipping out your computer. Insist that you want to show him a fabulous new website (www.whydontyouleavenow.com, perhaps?) and place your laptop in front of him. The energy from the computer should have him hurrying to the door in no time.

**'Give him the boot by whipping out your computer.'**

# How to become more popular

*Forget signing up for a million and one new evening classes. The easy way to improve your popularity rating is to raise your yang energy. This active energy is crucial for a buzzing social life, and to increase it in a jiffy you must start subtly redecorating your home. Place some red lights or red or yellow lanterns or lampshades in the south-west corner of your house and watch those invitations to glittering social events stack up on the doormat. Another guaranteed trick is to scatter your abode with sun symbols – paintings, ornaments, whatever – yet another excellent source of yang.*

Alternatively, write your wishes for more friends on a yellow banner and hang it from your roof. The wind will produce an energy that will see your wishes float off into the ether. Keep it there for at least a week and don't tell anyone what it's about, then burn it when you finally take it down.

**'Write your wishes on a yellow banner and hang it from your roof.'**

Oh, and try to cultivate friends of both sexes since this will beautifully balance the yin-yang energies. If you are a girl's girl, take an interest in the formerly yawn-worthy world of football or rugby; lads should likewise attempt to get in touch with their feminine side, however well hidden it may be. It's easy when you know how.

## Become the consummate gift giver

Good presents mean great success and happy faces all round. As Dickens said, to paraphrase wildly, there is really not much difference between giving and receiving since both parties reap the benefits. But what to give? Goldfish are super-lucky, partly due to their colour (gold signifies wealth and red happiness) and partly because fish symbolize success. Eight goldfish in particular are seen as especially lucky, but only if the bowl contains one black one to absorb any negativity. Never, ever give anyone an angel fish – unless they are your sworn enemy – because the sharp edges on the fins make them inauspicious pets.

Another symbol of good fortune is a plum blossom, making this the perfect gift-giving flower, although for extra good luck you should ensure that it is in full bloom. If you are in a particularly generous mood and fancy giving jewellery, make sure it is turquoise – this is the gem that signifies friendship. In any case, jewellery is bound to go down better than a fish.

## Wreak your revenge at weddings

Sigh … your oldest and dearest friend is becoming a Mrs – but you don't approve of the groom. The solution? Remove any good luck from the chapel. In China, a bride wears red because the yang energy is seen as being super-auspicious on the big day, and many of the guests do the same. You, however, should do the opposite – make sure there isn't a stitch of red on your clothing, and make sure as many other guests as possible to the same. But if you approve of the groom and want the marriage to work, have a word with him about his gift-giving skills. According to feng shui, a

**'Avoid wearing red, at all costs.'**

groom should give his bride four special presents to represent a long and fruitful life together. He'll thank you for this – and ensure you never stray from their Christmas card list.

- A bunch of pretty peonies, to represent marital happiness
- A box of good-quality chocolates, to represent a sweet life together
- A painting that includes both a child and a fish, to represent successful childbirth (wish him luck on finding one of these!)
- A gilt-edged mirror to protect their marriage from sha chi

## Matrimonial motors

Yes, yes, yes, we all know about attaching tin cans to the boot and spraying foam all over the paintwork, but what of the car that actually takes the bride to the ceremony?

First of all, the car should be red – the luckiest colour and the one most likely to produce lots of positive yang energy. Also, it should never, ever break down, be involved in an accident or even stall because this is incredibly inauspicious.

If this happens, however, and you approve of the marriage, you … as the ever-helpful guest and friend, can come to the rescue. Simply swing a curved knife through the air three times, going from right to left and left to right. You will have saved the day by overpowering any negative sha chi – just don't be surprised if other guests are reluctant to sit next to you later.

## A perfect present for a friend who's travelling

One of the members of your social set is off travelling the world and throws a party before departing for pastures new. You want to turn up with the ultimate gift, one that will help them on their way and, of course, ensure that you remain the key friend in his or her thoughts. The solution? Give them a conch shell.

Not only is this a traditional symbol of protection while travelling, but it will also help them meet interesting people on the way. The kind of people, in fact, to whom they will be waxing lyrical about their 'great friend who gave me this conch shell'. Fingers crossed.

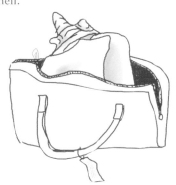

## Your very own good-luck talisman

With all this good luck you've been doling out – for your own ulterior motives, of course – you had better not forget your own good luck. The best way to safeguard your own success is to place a statue of a toad in your home, preferably near the front door. A three-legged toad is the symbol of wealth, health and happiness. Four legs, however, is not so good – it might look a little less odd but will not nearly be as auspicious.

### Never neglect your crystals

Continuing with the subject of personal good luck symbols, never take your crystals for granted. Crystals, of which you will now have many (you remember what brilliant talismans they are, don't you?), require a certain amount of TLC to ensure that they continue dishing out good fortune. They will need recharging once a week, so leave them in the sun for a couple of hours to destroy any negative sha chi. You should only ever display crystals that are 100 per cent natural. Ideally, hang seven different types in the south-west corner of your living room.

'Place a statue of a toad in your home.'

'Only display crystals that are 100% natural.'

New crystals must be introduced into your life with suitable reverence, namely by soaking them in water and sea salt for seven days and seven nights before placing them in direct sunlight to dry. Crystals: not as simple as you thought, are they?

### ... And get your hands on your enemy's ...

And sully them. One should never display crystals that are less than super-shiny, so make sure your enemy's are mucky. It is also extremely bad luck to have someone else touch your crystals because this will leave a residue of negative vibes, so fondle your enemy's as much as you can and watch with glee as their fortunes are reversed.

### Eliminating enemies

Before you start creating mischief, get ahead of the game by deducing whether your enemy is a yin or yang person. Everyone's personality veers towards an extreme based on the concept of the yin-yang symbol, a pair of intertwining black and white half-circles, each containing a dot of the corresponding colour.

- A yin person is passive, easygoing, thoughtful, laidback
  – indeed, maybe a little too chilled.

**Quick-fix outmanoeuvre trick**: Hide their wind chimes. Suddenly their world will seem topsy-turvy and out of control.

- A yang person is active, ambitious, decisive, a go-getter
  and maybe, well, a little uptight.

**Quick-fix outmanoeuvre trick**: Hack into their electronic organizer and rearrange their important dates. They are nothing without a set-in-stone schedule.

## Give bad gifts

Oh, the joy of gift giving! It's such a universal joy, in fact, that no one will realize your true intention is to hex them. Unlucky presents are sharp, pointy ones. A Swiss army knife, perhaps, or a corkscrew or pair of scissors (hey, who would be happy with these, anyway?). The theory goes that the sharp edges produce copious amounts of bad energy, namely sha chi, that will prove endlessly unlucky to the recipient.

The same principle works for plants, so if you're giving floral offerings to an enemy, aim for spiky leaves – cacti are particularly unlucky. Need the perfect excuse? Say you have just returned from Mexico and the sight of all those fabulous cacti inspired you. Dwarf plants are similarly unlucky because they symbolize stunted growth. This may be a bit too mean for some people, but could work very well on nasty exes.

## How to make sly Trojan horse-style offerings

The best inauspicious gifts are, of course, the ones that look harmless. The ones that make you, the generous donor, appear whiter than white. Present your enemy with a 'calming' picture of a waterfall or babbling brook. The end result will

'Your enemy will be infected by a cold.'

cook up a storm if you insist that they hang it in their bedroom. Water-related symbols usually bring about good fortune until they are introduced to the bedroom, where they will instantly usher in illness. As if by magic, your enemy will be infected by a cold they'll find impossible to shake off.

Another fantastically inauspicious gift is a blue heart pendant. Claim that the heart is a symbol that represents your friendship and he or she should wear it at all times. Ha! In truth, a blue heart symbolizes short-lived romances. Your false friend will have no idea why all their relationships have the lifespan of a week. As for you and the humble blue heart pendant, no one would suspect that for a second. Besides, who can resist a gift of jewellery?

## Revenge on friends who claim everyone fancies them

These are the ones (usually girls) who have the gall to insist that the whole world fancies the pants off them – including, no doubt, your boyfriend. Of course they are wrong – and hideously jealous, insecure creatures – but that won't stop them.

Something that will, though, is the following trick. On the final night of Chinese New Year, it is traditional for unmarried women to throw juicy oranges into a river to bring about a husband. Oranges are considered auspicious because the word for orange – 'kum' – is the same as the word for gold. While throwing the orange, the single gal must close her eyes and visualize her ideal man-to-be.

**'Influence the future love prospects of an enemy.'**

It's easy to relate this tradition to your false friend by insisting that she join you and replacing her juicy oranges with pithy, hollow ones. Better still, tell her that lemons are even more lucky and will make all the men in town fall instantly at her feet (although she already claims they have, but there you go). If her past behaviour is anything to go by, she will grab them off you and start hurling them in. With any luck, her future love prospects will be as bitter as the fruit.

## Tea with the mother-in-law

As gritting-your-teeth duties go, this ranks very near the top – but that doesn't mean you can't have some fun. She's coming round for tea, then? Well, serve her from a pot whose spout menacingly points directly at her and give the dragon lady a dose of her own medicine.

Alternatively, up the ante
a notch and why not give
her a chipped china cup
to drink from. Serving
and drinking out of
broken crockery brings

very bad luck – not to mention a host of nasty germs. Wouldn't it be
just dreadful if she felt unwell and had to cut short her stay?

## Dealing with house pests

House guests you don't want over, or ones who have outstayed their
welcome (when a couple of nights becomes a couple of weeks, say),
turn into house pests. Think you'll never be able to get rid of them?
Here's a sneaky solution: put them in a room with an en suite bathroom
and make sure their bed is directly opposite the toilet – the stagnant,
unmoving water in the bowl will produce sha chi (negative chi) and
they'll be having nightmares in no time.

Another sha chi conduit is an electric blanket. Pretend that you're doing
your guest an enormous favour by keeping him or her snug at night. In
truth, you will be doing the opposite because
the electromagnetic field produced by the
blanket is far from favourable in the bedroom.
Cue more nightmares!

**'Produce
negative chi.'**

If the above is still not making them move on, suggest they go to bed
in a room with overhead beams. The beams will create too much yang
energy, making it impossible to get a good night's sleep. The result:

headaches, tension and, if they're a couple, a feeling that they ought to separate. That should get them out of your hair!

## Wreak revenge on your nemesis' love prospects

So, there's a man you like but he fancies your sworn enemy. Don't let him know that the two of you don't get along – men are guaranteed to run a mile at the first sign of bitchiness. Instead, pretend that the two of you are the best of friends, and that you want to help him win her over. Suggest that he send her romantic red roses, but make sure the thorns are intact. As well as being a positive colour, red can also symbolize death and, in combination with the spiky stems, will ensure that their relationship never gets off the ground. Result!

Now that the object of your desire has given up on her, he will hopefully turn his attention to you. State how much you hate red roses – how hackneyed! how clichéd! – and how you believe yellow ones are much more chic, especially with the thorns removed. This combination is incredibly auspicious and will guarantee you both a long and happy future together. Double result!

## Annoying neighbours

We've all been there. The neighbour who plays techno all night long. Or the neighbour who insists on stone-cladding the front of their house, causing every other property in the street to drop in value. Or the neighbour who interferes with your private life.

Dealing with annoying neighbours is actually very easy because you can turn your home and garden into weapons. One way is to put up a

sharp or spiked fence. This doesn't have to
be anything as obvious as barbed wire –
even the most innocuous of picket fences
can cause mischief thanks to those spiky
ends (who would have thought suburbia
could be swimming in so much bad chi?).
Then top off the fence with a pointed arrow and
triangle directed at their house for an extra dose
of bad luck.

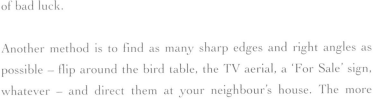

Another method is to find as many sharp edges and right angles as
possible – flip around the bird table, the TV aerial, a 'For Sale' sign,
whatever – and direct them at your neighbour's house. The more
'invisible' poison arrows aimed at them, the better.

A word of warning, though: make sure your nasty neighbour doesn't
practice feng shui or – worse still – invite a master round to suss out
why they are suddenly so unlucky. If they discover that you've been
besieging them with arrows, a full-scale
war could ensue with your neighbour
planting strategically placed mirrors to
reflect the bad luck back to you. Which is
the last thing you want.

**'A full-scale war could ensue with your neighbour.'**

### Bathroom-based sabotage

For more instantaneous results, you need to gather your nerves, bite
your tongue and actually go next door to confront your neighbour. Ask
to use their toilet – claim that yours is currently being fixed by a

plumber, or some such nonsense – and then quite literally lift the lid on your neighbour's misfortune by leaving the seat up. Feng shui masters go loopy over the powers of the humble lavatory because they believe that the toilet bowl acts as an urn, attracting any circulating chi. When you flush the toilet or leave the lid up, all beneficial chi instantly vanishes – as will your neighbour's good fortunes.

## How to feng shui your house after an argument

Obviously, you don't want any of that negative energy hanging around your house. Remove bad chi instantly with a quick cleanse of your home. Sprinkle a handful of sea salt on the floor of the room where the argument took place. Salt in feng shui terms acts rather like salt does in real life – namely, as a substance that absorbs surrounding moisture. According to feng shui, salt attracts any negative chi energy that may be circulating. Leave it overnight and vacuum it up the following morning, then repeat as necessary until all the bad vibes have dispersed. This trick also helps with moving on from any bad relationship – friendship, sexual, whatever – leaving you refreshed with positive energy ... and ready to create your mischief all over again!

'Hang the right kind of painting
in the boardroom and that
deal could be yours.'

# Chapter Three
# Success and Failure

*We spend a great chunk of our lives locked away in offices and chained to work stations, but most of us never really get the hang of office politics. This is a shame since there are so many sly and borderline ruthless ways of boosting our career prospects, especially if we use feng shui to aid our strategy. By now you know all too well that the presence of a humble goldfish can instantly increase your creativity and productivity, but did you also know that a stealthy reshuffle of someone's desk – that interfering PA who always questions your 'sick days', for example – will put her in a foul mood for the rest of the week? Or that there are ingenious tricks to get your boss in that all-important cheery mood around Christmas bonus time, or cunning plans on where to place people – and indeed objects – in a boardroom? Hang the right kind of picture, for instance, and that deal could be yours; sit facing the most auspicious direction and you will suddenly rival Bill Clinton for moving rhetoric. Office politics are all about game playing and power play tactics, about making the right moves at the right time, so with some sneaky oriental wisdom, you will be jumping from lowly intern to CEO in no time. Best of all, none of your colleagues will fathom how, exactly, your rise was so meteoric.*

# Eliminate the office competition

*Think a desk is nothing more than a place to stack papers and store your computer? Think again. Your desk is the best way to start wreaking office havoc with some subtle nasty feng shui. For starters, you must be able to walk around the desk in a full circle without any obstruction; that way, the chi will have sufficient space to breath and circulate freely. The perfect desk also has very specific measurements. A desk that is 60-61 inches long will result in an increase in power luck; one that is 40-42 inches wide means mentor luck; and if it is 33 inches high, you will be overwhelmed with money luck. Sawing the legs off your old desk, then, could result in a massive pay rise.*

Next, whip out a compass and work out your desk's different directions. To be super-canny, put a goldfish bowl in the northern corner – this is the area associated with your career, and goldfish are lucky because of their colour: red for success, gold for money. Cannier still is a black or blue fish, symbolic of metal and water, also important for your career. A wind chime can help, too. Again, make sure it is metal because this is the element that most helps with work-related matters, and also that it's hollow to ensure that the chi flows freely.

If your colleagues don't already think you have gone mad, what with your requests for fish and wind chimes, ask if it's possible to paint your office space green. According to Chinese tradition, this is the perfect colour for easing tired eyes, giving you that crucial edge you need to succeed. Oooh, how ruthless!

**'Ask to paint your office green.'**

## Desk accessories to get ahead

To get one step ahead of the office competition, think carefully about what you have on your desk – the right accessories could see you rising up the ranks in no time. Your desk lamp should be curved and ergonomic – you want nothing angular on your desktop, even a lamp, as the sharp edges are guaranteed to create poison arrows that pierce your good fortune. Desk lamps are also beneficial because you should never have the sole source of light above your head – this, supposedly, puts too much pressure on your head and shoulders, resulting in even more stress than usual.

A computer, for once, is actually good for you – well, in feng shui terms, since all that energy makes you more productive. However, an office full of buzzing work stations – ie, your average office – will create too much energy, so soften this with plants. Some properly placed foliage will also absorb any invisible poison arrows from office furniture, not known for its soft lines. But avoid placing plants in the northern quarter, the area most associated with your career, because they will soak up water, the necessary element for this work. Don't let any of these plants die, particularly any in the south-east corner, because this will cause financial ruin.

The south-east corner also represents communication, making this the perfect place for your phone. The west is best for finance, so put your wallet and cheque book here and you might receive an unexpected bonus. The south, on the other hand, represents public recognition, making this the perfect corner for showing off any awards you might have won – that's if your colleagues don't already hate you enough. In the southern corner, hang a picture of something that will motivate you to work harder and earn more money – a shiny red Porsche, perhaps, or a luxury break in palm-fringed Bali. This image will motivate you and encourage you, Gordon Gekko-like, to believe that lunch is for wimps. You will soon be working harder than you ever thought possible. Yikes!

**'West is best for finance.'**

### An empty desk equals an empty mind?

Perhaps, but a cluttered, messy, paper-strewn work space unquestionably clouds your head. To solve this, declutter the area around your desk, especially at floor level. Try to ensure that any wires from computers and the like don't criss-cross. If they do, this could create opposing energies that may conflict. Also make sure that you don't have bookcases with open shelves because these sharp edges create a

mass of poison arrows. Instead, have cupboards or use doors to hide the offending corners.

**'Disperse the stagnant chi.'**

Next, turn your attention to your in-tray and rifle regularly through the piles of papers to disperse the stagnant chi. This may be more productive than actually getting all your work done.

## Where to sit to get success

The ideal office should have revolving doors at the entrance to ensure an ease of flow for the chi as well as an effective way of deflecting any poison arrows. This luck affects your entire office, though – remember, you need to adopt a more selfish frame of mind and start protecting number one.

The ideal direction for your desk chair should be east because this is best for concentration. However, as your mood and indeed your requirements change throughout the working day, it might be wise to move your chair around

**'Adopt a more selfish frame of mind.'**

to reap the necessary benefits. When you face west, you will find it easiest to focus on a difficult task, while north is perfect for getting a new perspective on an old issue. If you are desperate to attract someone's attention – maybe your boss's so he or she will finally realize how gloriously important and indispensable you are – position yourself with your chair to the south.

You will also need a 'power chair', one with a high back and solid arm rests, so leave those funny-shaped posture-improving chairs to the kind of people who care more about health than promotion – the wimps. Ensure that your chair is in the 'command' position – in other words, the position farthest from the door with your back to the wall. That way, you can counteract any backstabbing, metaphorical or otherwise.

## Evil entrances

Become a door bore and ensure that the entrance and exit to your office directs all that good chi to you – and no one else. Doors can prove a problem. You categorically don't want an office with two doors because all the good chi coming in one door will fly straight out of the other. You must also never have a desk where you are sitting with your back to the door or to a window – all your luck will leave and there will be nothing you can do to stop it.

'Direct all that good chi to yourself.'

Talking of windows, inward opening windows are considered extremely bad for careers and offices in general. Thank goodness, then, for air conditioning and hermetically sealed windows that could never open inwards even if prised with an axe.

# How to transform your boss into a simpering slave

*Give the right kind of gifts to your boss and success is guaranteed. Think of it as the grown-up version of the teacher's pet and the apple. Want to break some news they are guaranteed to hate? About to ask for a pay rise? A present should soften the blow and make them agree to anything. It is crucial that you choose the right gift, though: a tried-and-tested feng shui favourite is the plum blossom, but only when the flower is in full bloom – check first for any unopened buds.*

Another top tip is to place a small statuette of an elephant on your desk. This symbolizes wisdom, something that usually comes with years of experience. This subtle ornament is actually your fast track to office swami-dom. Sooner or later, your boss will be seeking your advice on everything from promotions to what they should sell in the staff canteen. Since it's lonely at the top, he or she will see you as their sole confidante, giving you even more opportunity to work your nasty corporate feng shui.

# Dress for success

*Power dressing didn't disappear with the Eighties. Oh no, it lives on in double-breasted pinstripe suits, spike-heeled stilettos and shoulder pads that go on for miles. It's true that you should dress for the job you want, not the job you have, and feng shui can help you dress appropriately and outshine the competition.*

For a start, don't wear black – a shocking revelation indeed since this is the preferred shade for most workers, but in fact this is the colour that will drain you of energy. Black also deflects decisions, so people will ignore you and talk over you – you don't want to become the office doormat, do you? However, you can wear black as long as it's not head-to-toe noir, so team it with another colour, preferably red or purple. These are the power shades, but don't overdo them because they are also associated with anger, both from the wearer and those around him or her.

Feng shui power dressing also requires the right kind of accessorizing. Lapis and amethysts are both associated with power and being in control, so these are great gems for jewellery that doubles as secret amulets to help you get ahead. Think carefully about your scent, too. Sage is a power scent because it produces clarity and focus, as does rosemary. Don't overdo either, though, or you could end up smelling like the Sunday roast, which is not the kind of impact you want to make.

The ultimate power outfit, believe it or not, is an ensemble with a nautical theme. The reckoning behind this wisdom is that a naval look will allow the chi to flow freely, supposedly like a sailboat in the wind, so dress like Popeye and success will be yours. Perhaps.

# Sneaky strategies to see off the office competiton

*Everyone has one — an office nemesis, someone you are convinced is after your job, who you tolerate with a tight smile — but luckily it is simple to outwit him or her. An undercover solution is to start wearing pointy shoes, the more wicked and witch-like, the better. The sharp footwear acts as daggers that you can surreptitiously direct at your enemy. Hey presto! Instant invisible poison arrows to damage their good chi. Of course, this works best with women — men in pointy shoes may be asked why they've started dressing that way.*

Alternatively, clutter up the object of your loathing's desk. This will bring stagnant chi to their work space – oh, and baffle them, which will consequently wreck their day. Get in early and make a habit of some sneaky stealth-ruffling before the work day begins.

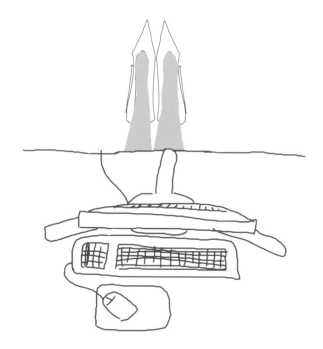

# How to get ahead in meetings

*Nothing can be more nerve-wracking than chairing a difficult meeting, perhaps one that could result in a lucrative deal, which in turn will do your reputation wonders.*

Certain factors can ease your important meeting. For a start, make sure you're sitting in the right place. Reserve the plum position at the conference table for you: namely, the seat in the 'command' position with a wall behind and an uninterrupted view of the door. This not only ensures that any positive chi will be directed your way, but also means you can keep an eye on any comings or goings to and from the room. Conversely, never, ever sit with your back to the door – this is very unlucky and you will subsequently spend the entire meeting on the edge of your seat.

**'Any positive chi will be directed your way.'**

The right kind of picture may also help you to clinch that deal. A dragon on the right-hand side of the door facing your seat will give you the strength to dazzle your audience and hypnotize the boardroom into believing your every word.

Also, think about your outfit. Blue is associated with good communication, while yellow represents clarity and wisdom. A canary yellow suit, then, could wow your subjects into submission.

# Attract others to you

*So you've got a new job, which in turn calls for a new image. Now's your chance to create a mystique, an aura of greatness. What are you going to do? Wear a hat! Yes, honestly – all eyes will automatically look at you, your colleagues will find you inexplicably mesmerizing, and simply because of some clever headgear.*

Another tip is to put a bright light in the southern section of your desk. This ensures instant fame, and thus a cult-like following. Soon you will be the person everyone in the office looks up to – and with that kind of power, you can do anything.

# Guard your reputation

*As investment guru Warren Buffett once said, 'It takes twenty years to build a reputation and five minutes to ruin it.' Guard yours with your life – since you're not only directing all that bad chi at others, you also need to protect yourself from being infected by their misfortune, distancing yourself while simultaneously looking like you're not doing so. So complex!*

**'Transform your desk into a cocoon of safety.'**

One way is to adopt an office talisman. Traditional feng shui symbols of good luck will help – for instance, the three-legged toad or the double happiness symbol, preferably made from jade. Both items can be bought from most Chinese supermarkets – ask for help if you're unsure of the symbol – and are easy to display discretely on your desk.

To safeguard your reputation even further, check the window nearest your desk for secret poison arrows – in other words, any right angles or sharp edges like the side of a roof that point directly at you or your desk. Deflect these swiftly with strategically placed eight-sided ba gua mirrors (found in most oriental markets) – again, these can be small and discrete. Congratulations! You have transformed your desk into a cocoon of safety.

## Keep your friends close – and your enemies closer

This is an old adage, but one that still rings true. The most effective way to draw an enemy in is to befriend them. Or rather, become a false office friend. Make a grand gesture pertaining to newfound friendship by presenting your enemy with a gift. A plant is perfect; any type is fine. However – and this part is crucial – insist that they place it in the northern corner of their desk. This should sap away any water in this quarter, the necessary element for career success. In other words, the placing of the plant will hinder their prospects. Be careful, though – plants in other areas of the desk are lucky – they will encourage the flow of chi, and thus aid your enemy's success. Which is obviously the last thing you want.

Another form of mild treachery is to scuff up your nemesis' shoes. This can be done in an oh-so-subtle manner, such as accidentally treading on their toes when you're leaving the office lifts. Scuffed-up shoes are said to reflect damage to the soul. Your boss should subconsciously take note and rule them out for future promotions.

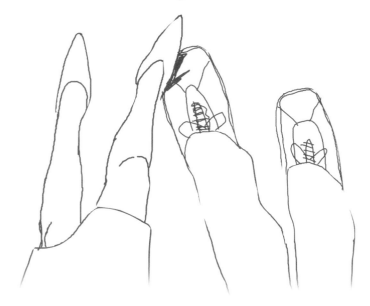

## How a photocopier could prove your secret weapon

That stalwart of the office, the humble photocopier, could actually prove your staunchest ally, as long as you place it in the correct spot. Confused? Don't be – the powers of the photocopier are simple enough. Basically, in the same way that a photocopier quickly heats up when in use, the machine will overheat any circulating chi – and you don't want burnt chi near you. Insist that the photocopier be moved towards a door near your office nemesis – maybe use a sneaky health excuse and claim that your doctor has diagnosed you with the highly unusual overexposure-to-photocopiers syndrome. Everything will start going wrong for your nemesis – and he or she will have no protection to fall back on. Oh dear!

# Dictate office romance

*Since you spend so much of your time in the office, you might as well develop an office crush to help wile away the hours. Besides, the work place is the perfect location to meet someone of the opposite sex — at the very least, you will have mutual conversation pointers for your first date.*

If you're sick of hanging around the water cooler waiting for love to blossom organically, you may need to take action and start actively cultivating romance. First, try to work in a room that faces north-west with a door that faces south-east. These two auspicious directions will instantly make you irresistible to men — or women — and in no time at all you will be the office babe.

Also, take care over the east corner of your desk or work space because this is the quarter associated with office romance. The sexy sector will need to be stirred up with something that signifies passion and the fire element, so place something suitable, such as a red light or — if that creates raised eyebrows from your colleagues — a picture of a volcano. In no time at all, you will be getting all manner of suggestive emails.

# Be the consummate team player

*In management-speak, this is what every company looks for in an employee: someone willing to join in and work as part of a team, someone who won't rock the boat.*

The best way to ensure that you become the consummate team player is to study your sleeping conditions. Look at your bedroom ceiling – are you sleeping under a beam? If you are, this is inauspicious. You will instantly be blamed for the mistakes of others and will also get migraines – which, of course, makes you less productive and less likely to pull your weight.

However, there is a solution. The ideal answer is to create a false ceiling over the beam. If this is unfeasible – feng shui has a habit of being impractical unless you want to spend thousands remodelling your house – hang bamboo stalks from the beam, tied with red ribbon for added luck. Bingo! You will suddenly become an indispensable member of your office.

## And the ultimate, unforgiving risk-taker

Research consistently proves that maverick risk takers do best in business, so take a deep breath and start taking more risks.

Risk takers need to choose their desk decoration with care. Eschew pictures of your family or pets in favour of a mountain. If you are about to take risks, the idea is to aim high and the mountain will remind you of this. You can make the picture of the mountain less obvious if you prefer, perhaps disguising it as

**'Start taking more risks.'**

an innocent holiday snap of you standing by the Alps. This will also
ensure that anyone else in the picture's line of vision will not start
usurping you by taking even more risks.

Another aid for risk taking is to wear a dragon. This potent symbol of
power also signifies courage. Wear a discrete dragon every day – maybe
as a tie clip or a brooch. In fact, the dragon is particularly good for
women because it instantly ups their quota of masculine yang energy.

# How to get a pay rise

*This is a tricky one because a pay rise or a bonus ought to be down to hard work that's justly rewarded. No? Of course not! First, add symbols of wealth to your desk – gold or antique coins tied with red ribbon are particularly effective. These symbols will bring about monetary success as well as safeguard you from financial ruin.*

The south-east sector is also important because this area represents your personal wealth. Water symbolizes wealth and prosperity, so add as much of this element here as possible – think a fountain or fish pond. On a smaller, more discrete and quite frankly office-friendly scale, a picture of a waterfall or a babbling brook will suffice. The continual flow of water represents the constant flow of chi and thus auspicious monetary luck. Donald Trump is particularly fond of indoor water features in the south-east sector of Trump Towers – and just look where some nifty feng shui has got him.

## Get rich quick

Okay, so you've secured that pay rise, but greedy-old-you wants more. To get properly rich, turn your sights homeward and make your house as lucky as possible. Start with some basic home maintenance and fix any leaking taps – this will stop money from pouring out of your house.

Next, take note of your home's sources of heat. If you have a fireplace, a boiler or even an oven in the west or north-west sector, put some artists' charcoal (that black stuff you'll find in any artists' store) in a ceramic pot near the source of heat – and thus fire – to neutralize the mix of energies. The north and north-west areas are concerned with money and career, and only really respond well to the element of water.

To get richer still, you need to be flash with your cash. Place the largest denomination note of your currency tied with a lucky red ribbon in the west corner of your house. The west represents the setting sun and harvest time, and therefore the fruits of your labour. You should also put a safe, if you have one, in this part of your home.

Another directional matter worth remembering is that the south-west sector is associated with saving money, so put yellow flowers here to make sure you stop frittering away any hard-earned cash.

# How to start your own business

*Frankly, since most new businesses fail within a year of starting up, you will need all the help you can get. In China, owners of new start-ups always consult a feng shui master to ensure that everything is auspiciously on their side. The single most important factor is the location. A T-junction is considered extremely inauspicious, as indeed is a business located close to a flyover – the sharp, cutting shape of the fast-moving road produces sharp, cutting chi. However, a business that overlooks a roundabout is very lucky – all that circulating chi will churn out lots of luck. Similarly, a business in a location with lots of gently downward-sloping roads leading towards it is a very good thing but, if the roads are too steep, the chi will come tumbling down too fast and cause no end of grief.*

Your compass will also come in handy here. Get your bearings and place your cash till in the south-west corner. Better still, place a mirror opposite, symbolically doubling your takings. If possible your sign or logo should be in the south-east corner and, if you can, incorporate something lucky into the design. Maybe a lucky number, in fact, so read on.

## Ruthless strategies

The Chinese are very hot on lucky numbers and will automatically reject cars with inauspicious number plates and even houses with unlucky addresses.

The luckiest number for anyone with their own business is eight, since this is the number most associated with being rich. You should

**'The luckiest number is eight.'**

therefore incorporate as many aspects of eight as possible into your business to increase your luck – eight-sided tables, eight flowers and so on. Many Chinese businesses have a fish tank for luck, and it is more than likely that the tank will include eight goldfish plus one black fish to quash any negative chi that might have entered the bowl. Alternatively, wear a fish brooch.

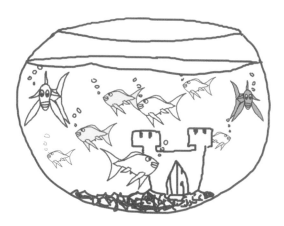

Other lucky numbers include six, which symbolizes wealth, five for harmony, nine for longevity and two for ease. You can even mix and match numbers for a combination of luck: 26 means easy wealth, for instance, while 58 should bring both harmony and riches.

Never be tempted with the number four. This is the most inauspicious of numbers and is said to represent death, so avoid anything

**'Avoid anything that comes in fours at all costs.'**

that comes in fours at all costs. Indeed, don't even think about relocating your business to an address containing the number four, however popular the road.

## Make your decor work for you

Finally, while you are sifting through the paint charts and fabric swatches, don't forget the feng shui principles of decorating. The ideal space should be the perfect balance of yin and yang. In other words, mix light and shade, include all of the different elements – while allowing no single one to overwhelm the others – and combine the right kind of colours. Blue, green and white are all considered calming yin colours, for instance, while red and yellow are dynamically yang.

Also invest in some good luck symbols. Admittedly, these are far from tasteful – and therefore tricky if you're hoping to open a style bar, say, or a chi chi boutique – but these talismans will protect you from outside evils. A pair of temple lions, male and female Fu dogs, should come in particularly handy. If placed on either side of the entrance, these dogs will act as guardians, protecting your business from outside evil influences and frightening away bad luck while ushering in future prosperity.

**'Talismans will protect you from outside evils.'**

## Banish your corporate competitor to the basement

The best way to ensure your business rival instantly loses his magic touch? Banish him to the basement. The best offices, feng shui-wise, are those at the top of a building – light, bright and with plenty of windows (albeit ones with a distinct lack of 'poison arrows'). Great for you, then, if you're fortuitous to have one of these offices, not so great if your competitor is up there and you're hoping to quash him. So persuade him that working in a basement is more productive – surveys prove it! (of course they don't … but lie) – due to the lack of stimuli. In reality, working in a windowless room spells business doom. The lack of a view – and, very often, human contact – swiftly leads to a feeling of being out of touch and, well, lacking in vision. In every sense.

'Park in the corner of the car park
and spend the rest of the day
under a dark cloud.'

# Chapter Four

# Health and Misfortune

*After all this machiavellian mischief, you'd better start guarding your own luck. If someone gets a whiff of what you have been up to, they'll have the protective mirrors out in no time, reflecting all that bad energy back at you. Some people are born lucky. Others make their own luck, the clever ones using nasty feng shui. Hundreds of years ago, only the emperor was allowed to practise feng shui; anyone else found dabbling was immediately sentenced to death. These emperors were shrewd fellows: they knew that not only is feng shui an excellent way of improving one's own luck, but that it's also a sure means of destroying the luck of others. Did you know, for instance, that by subtly repositioning your TV aerial, you could drive out those annoying neighbours? Or if you encourage your office nemesis to park in the corner of the car park, they'll spend the rest of the day under a dark cloud? Talking of which, you must remember to protect your own health, too, especially since keeping in tip-top shape means you'll always stay one step ahead of the game – crucial in the art of nasty feng shui.*

# Make your home a fortress

*Your luck starts on your doorstep. By treating your home as your castle, you should be able to keep your enemies at arm's length. As you probably now realize, feng shui starts in the home — by rejigging your furniture and the like — so by protecting your house, you're automatically protecting your luck, leaving you more time to misbehave.*

## Location, location, location

That old estate agent's adage is all the more true when it comes to feng shui and guarding your luck. Where you live rules how lucky you are, and how likely your naughty pranks are to pay off.

Never live in a house with a church spire aligned with your front door – the straight line instantly becomes a conduit of sha chi, or bad energy. The same thing will happen if you live near a viaduct or overhead train line – plus the view will hardly be to-die-for – or if you have a straight line pointing towards your house (a roundabout can deflect this). Also avoid living near a graveyard – all that cutting chi from those crosses doesn't bear thinking about. It's good news if you live in a cul-de-sac but – BUT – bad news if your house is at the end because all the other houses will steal your chi. Living near a hospital, prison, cemetery or abattoir is inauspicious because all these locations are too yin – and, let's face it, not that picturesque. If you do live near a cemetery, however, there is a solution: paint the wall facing the cemetery bright red and erect two tall spotlights between your house and the building. Not worth it? Then move, preferably to somewhere with a grand

**'Not worth it? Then move.'**

entrance. In an ideal feng shui world, your perfect house would have a circular driveway. Since beneficial chi moves in circles, lady luck will pay a visit in no time.

## L, no!

Say 'Hell, no!' to any Ls. Anything L-shaped acts as a wrench and will promptly fence you in, so avoid L-shaped sofas, rooms, houses, the lot. If you want feng shui luck, you need perfect balance, something you won't get from an L.

## Become a demon organiser

There are some scary people who are born project managers, who keep strict to-do lists and actually stick to them. The rest of us need all the help we can get, so invest in a massive, old-fashioned grandfather clock. The idea is that the loud, unavoidable ticking will bring more rhythm and therefore more order into your life, giving you more time, of course, to concentrate on making mischief. Another symptom, of course, is that it could drive you mad.

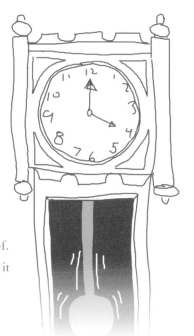

## A godsend for gold diggers

Think it's just Jane Austen girls who

want to marry into money? Not a chance: there are plenty of women today who choose money over love – at any cost. All you gold diggers should pay careful attention to your front door. Changing the position of the entrance to your house is the best way to change your general energy, your overall luck and – most importantly – your marriage prospects. North-facing front doors mean the residents are too fussy – this is the worst position to be in. The best is south. Moving the position, however, is not as hard as you might think: simply build a porch or a screen to redirect the chi.

You want to marry into wealth? Aim for a north-west door – interestingly just a notch away from inauspicious north, so make sure you read those compass directions with care. Beware, though: a north-west door can also mean you're a ruthless social climber. However, if you're a gold digger, you probably are, aren't you?

## Become a crazed declutterer

Remember how great you feel after a thorough spring clean? How that purging effect works wonders on the soul? Decluttering your house in feng shui terms produces a similar effect – times a thousand.

'Encourage clutter in other houses.'

Clutter or mess, however you wish to term it, accumulates stagnant chi. You could release that chi by reshuffling your clutter periodically, but it makes much more sense to have a permanently tidy and organized home. There should be no dark corners, so lighten them with a spotlight or a cleverly placed horse sculpture; a horse is a yang animal that will counteract all that yin.

In fact, your whole home should always be well lit, not only with a dearth of dark corners, but also no pokey little rooms – everything, in fact, should be light, bright and breezy. This will ensure years of excellent relationships since light represents yang, which in turn symbolizes happiness and success. Simple when you know how.

## Crafty circles equal a lucky living room

This is your space for entertaining others as well as chilling out, so think carefully about decor. For a start, you want to aim for lots of circles – to guide that circulating chi, remember. Invest in round tables and chairs with rounded backs – these will also minimize the chances of any 'secret arrows' bouncing off the right-angled edges. Leave the centre of the room clear with an empty circle-shaped space so that the chi can flow more freely – and you and any guests can dance more madly. The Chinese also consider rounded shapes symbolic of money, so your new rotund-related lounge could even make you richer. Bonus!

Your ornaments should be of the auspicious variety, so you'll need more crystals in your living room than Gypsy Rose Lee. To maximize their beneficial qualities, aim for a variety of types – at least seven. The luckiest are those with several facets that reflect lots of light. This light will create pretty rainbows that in turn promote a happy home.

Also, make your florist your best friend – fresh flowers bring beneficial chi to your house, though never leave them lingering when they start to wilt as dead plants signify death. Luckily, silk flowers work just as well, and of course never die – but remember to dust them regularly or they will become a source of stagnant chi.

Finally, sort out any square pillars. They cut chi – it's all those sharp edges again – in four directions at once. Soften square pillars by installing a climbing plant to neutralize the chi. But then, with pillars, where are you living? A castle?

## Paint your bedroom the right colour

Don't paint your bedroom red. Even one wall of scarlet can spell bad news because red in a bedroom – the most sensitive room to colour – means you will never be able to sleep. Instead, go for powder blue or lilac or a neutral colour like the usually dreaded magnolia.

'Paint your enemy's bedroom red!'

Oh, and avoid any red in the corridor or indeed staircase leading to your bedroom. Incidentally, the ideal staircase should be gently curving. A spiral staircase, on the other hand, represents a corkscrew-style piercing of the house. And one painted red? A piercing that has resulted in blood. Yikes!

## Pactice nasty feng shui and sleep soundly at night

Back to the bedroom: always sleep with your head pointing towards the door because this will ensure you have an uninterrupted night's sleep. If you're facing the other way, you're bound to wake up. Likewise, a mirror facing the bed will result in disturbed nights, as indeed will any pictures hanging behind your pillow or a large chandelier positioned over the bed frame – which makes sense: you're probably subconsciously worried that the darned thing is about to crush you.

## Make sure divorce doesn't happen to you

Unless you actually want to be single, never, ever have a double bed with two single mattresses – hey, this was never going to give you positive relationship luck, was it? This symbolizes separation and could lead to just that – and maybe even divorce. If you have different requirements when it comes to firmness, invest in a bespoke mattress that incorporates both of your wishes. Oddly enough, it's okay to have twin beds – well, okay in feng shui terms.

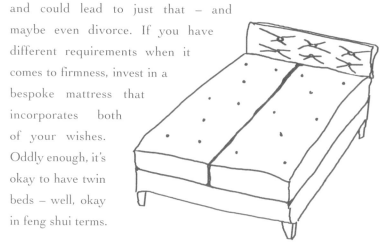

## Banish beams

Think beams are a characterful feature? Pah! The truth is that they press down on your luck as well as give you headaches, a bad night's sleep, you name it. If you can't create a false ceiling – or indeed, if you're reluctant to relinquish such a lovely feature from your home – hang bamboo sticks or a small wind

**'Forget beams and create a false ceiling.'**

chime from the offending beams to deflect any sha chi. Much depends on the type of beam. If they're decorative and therefore regular and part of a series, your beams will not nearly be as bad for you as the genuine old timber types beloved of traditional country pubs – in fact, these beams can actually break up bad chi.

**'Keep computers out.'**

One final thing to make sure you always get lucky in your bedroom is to keep computers out. Their buzzy electromagnetic fields will interrupt the concept of your bedroom as a sanctuary, and you will soon find sleeping a chore.

## The doors of doom

Make sure the door leading into your bedroom opens inwards – if it opens out, this will create quarrelsome energies. Since the bedroom can be the location for the most fearsome of quarrels, you want as much luck here as you can muster. Also, leave the door closed as often as possible – again, this will stop fights.

Still on the subject of doors, too many openings to the outside of your house will create tension – in feng shui terms, these excess doors are seen as an excess of mouths. Block off all doors except your main entrance.

## Cook up mischief in the kitchen

Although the bedroom is the most important room for ensuring a lifetime of good fortune, don't neglect the rest of your house, especially your kitchen. The powerful elements of fire and water are both strong here, so your sink and oven should never be opposite each other since

'Create conflict by putting the sink and oven opposite each other.'

these opposing elements create conflict. Appease them by introducing greenery and wooden features to your kitchen as a whole – fire needs wood and water loves foliage.

And, however convenient they may be, don't ever get buy a microwave – they create too much radiation and therefore too much chi. However, investing in an Aga could be a very wise decision: the natural flame element makes this an auspicious household object. Style-wise, forget aluminium and sleek marble surfaces and aim for the country kitchen look.

## Safeguard your bathroom

My, how those feng shui masters hate the bathroom! If it were up to them, we wouldn't have one at all and would instead spend our lives seeking out a convenient bush.

For starters, the bathroom should never be visible from the front door – these unlucky rooms are brilliant at losing all the lucky chi you've been attempting to generate and, if your bathroom is near your main entrance, it will fly out even faster still.

Your mirrors should never be placed so low as to cut off the head of the person reflected – as you would expect, this represents a beheading, which is so not a good look. And always – ALWAYS – keep the toilet lid down to stop any chi from escaping.

The colour white is okay here but don't go too white crazy in the rest of the house and create a monument to minimalism. White is too yin, so you'll need to balance it with plenty of bright sofas, paintings and rugs. Besides, that all-white look is so Nineties now.

## Adopt some nouveau style icons

It is extremely important that you adequately protect your front door because this is where the chi enters and leaves the house. You will therefore need some suitable guards. The Chinese recommend a pair of stone lions – how nouveau! – the traditional guardians of temples, on either side of the door. Umbrellas, another symbol of protection, outside your front door should also protect you from all the bad vibes your wicked feng shui has been giving out – and from burglars, too.

Another icon of nouveau chic is a kidney-shaped pool – much more lucky than a pool with sharp edges. However, avoid mirrored tiles. The resulting fractured images are unlucky for whoever is reflected – unless, of course, you want to put one in a guest bathroom you only reserve for your enemies. Just a thought ...

## Cunning coinage

For your final flourish, make your very own household talisman to boost your luck even more. Use old Chinese coins or, if you can't find any, coins collected from your travels tied together with red thread will do. These tied-together coins should bring you good luck – and lots of wealth. Hurrah!

## Get greedy with your green fingers

Forget masses of gravel and a few starved-looking geraniums – for feng shui luck, you need lots of lush foliage to accumulate positive chi. Better still, turn your garden into an Alpine forest – evergreens are fabulous accumulators because they never shed leaves.

> **'Turn your garden into an Alpine forest.'**

Have a curved, naturalistic, meandering path and lots of water features, especially round ponds since they collect chi. Don't forget the goldfish: you need eight gold ones and one black, remember, to neutralize any negative chi. Since you also need balance, introduce a touch of yang to your space with a stone statue or some polished rocks or pebbles.

Forget about being considerate to the environment – as you may have guessed by now, being 'green' is not exactly compatible with much of feng shui, even in the garden. A compost heap, then, is a very bad idea since all that rotting vegetation means too much yin. Sling your waste somewhere more auspicious – maybe over your nasty neighbour's fence?

**'Sling your rotting veg over your neighbour's fence.'**

## Move to Manhattan

Okay, this might be a drastic measure, but in feng shui terms, New York is considered extremely auspicious. You should always buy a house with a protective hill or mountain behind it; even a protective building will do. If this is not possible, plant a row of trees behind your building.

So why Manhattan? Because the tall skyscrapers – especially the Empire State Building – are considered 'mountains', and hence will automatically protect all the apartment buildings. Not only that, but Manhattan's many rivers are seen as chi-channelling waterways, the bridges that link the island to the mainland are regarded as 'heaven dragons' and the tunnels as 'earth dragons'. Dragons represent extreme good luck in feng shui – no wonder then that Manhattan property prices are so high.

## Sneaky subway success

Oh, and don't forget New York's subway stations – in fact, this applies to anywhere in the world with a metro system. The entrances are considered extremely lucky because you are close to the mouth of an earth dragon who lives underground, and are hence an auspicious place to live near. Remember this when you're next battling your way to work – be grateful you're taking public transport!

# How to make yourself invincible

*Okay, so you religiously drink three litres of water a day and have at least five portions of fruit and veg, but still you're always ill. Maybe you should be eating more peaches. Peaches represent good health and longevity – as indeed do bamboo, pine trees and cranes, so a few perfectly placed pictures representing these symbols should ensure that you're never poorly again.*

Also rethink your wardrobe. Both blue and green are healthy colours to wear, while white is known to destroy good health. Wow! Ever thought about telling your nemesis how much white suits them?

## Feng shui your way to gorgeousness

Well, at least your hair. Jennifer Lopez and Jerry Hall are devotees of feng shui-ing their luscious locks. Certain hairdressers, apparently, can read the direction your hair grows at the nape of the neck, and then create a style in harmony with this. Try it at home: suss out which way your hair grows, and accept it. In other words ditch those straighteners if a straight fringe is not your destiny. Harmony and balance – achieve that and you're sorted.

## Make people love you

The statistics say it all: married people live longer, have lower incidences of fatal diseases and are generally much healthier, so you'd better get hitched – and quick.

**'You'd better get hitched – quickly.'**

The instant solution for the perennially single starts at home. A single woman should make her house more yang and, conversely, a single man with a straight-from-central-casting bachelor pad should go more yin. Both can do this with the right symbolic ornaments – for a single girl, lots of dragons; for a man, plenty of phoenixes. And both should give up hope of ever being complimented on their interior good taste again.

Another decorating tip of questionable classiness is to adorn your home with as many double happiness symbols as you can stand. The Chinese symbol is lucky in all areas of life, but particularly when it comes to love. Get it engraved into your furniture, display it in paintings, even wear it as a pendant.

## How to ensure your enemy is unlucky in love

However, the double happiness symbol becomes incredibly unlucky if it's slept on or stepped upon. If you're looking for a gift for a not-so-favoured friend, tell them how auspicious the symbol is and then present them with a pillowcase or a rug – perfect for a dose of duplicity.

## Love spell one: use a balloon to ensure your beloved

Buy a bunch of helium balloons in auspicious colours – think reds, yellows, white and pinks. Using a felt-tipped pen, write down everything you're looking for in your perfect partner, allowing one wish/attribute per balloon. Let them float off on the breeze. The wind energy will stir up your wishes, speeding along their realization.

If you're doing this with a friend you don't like, hand over balloons in unlucky colours such as blues, greens and black. What a pity: they're single for longer than you!

'Hand over balloons in unlucky colours.'

## Love spell two: spawn the spouse of your dreams

This is for long-term love – ie, marriage – so treat this spell with the reverence it deserves. Make a list of everything you want in a partner – on the left-hand side, list all the qualities you'd like; on the right-hand side, all the not-so-nice qualities you'll tolerate. Deliberate carefully:

> **'No big breasts from men.'**

nothing on the list should be too light-hearted, so no big breasts from men and big wallets from women. Put the list in a gift box, tie it with red ribbon for extra yang energy and place the box in the south-west corner of your bedroom. Improve your chances by placing a series of paired objects by the box – a pair of mandarin ducks, for instance, are famous for their love-attracting qualities. Just make sure the ducks never separate.

## Puppy love

Single people should get a pet. Pets are like people because they create

positive chi. This is necessary if you're living alone because, frankly, you need all the help you can get in battling that negative chi solo. Don't get a parrot, though. In fact, caged birds of any kind are bad luck as they represent a lack of freedom.

## The benefits of babies

Don't be churlish when your favourite girlfriends become mothers. Instead, celebrate their babies' births by sending gifts made of gold – bangles, coins, whatever. In addition, throw the newborn babe a first-month party, with a fabulously elaborate dinner in an extravagantly decorated room. Your best friend will be overwhelmed with your good nature and generosity. Of course, all this in turn increases your own good fortune triple-fold.

## What to do with annoying neighbours

To safeguard your health, you need to watch your neighbours, especially the nasty ones. Here's what to do to keep them under your control:

1   **Become a guerrilla gardener**

Employ some light sabotage in your neighbour's garden by destroying their carefully cultivated rock garden, especially if it's situated in the south-west corner. This is the area that represents relationships, so a rock garden here will strengthen the earth energy. Replace the garden with some evil-looking rocks. The Chinese believe that rocks have personalities, so find ones that look suitably threatening and devilish to further their misfortune.

You could also offer to cut down their dead tree and leave a stump – this will attract tonnes more stagnant chi to their now incredibly inauspicious garden.

2   **Forget cable: get a satellite dish!**

And point the monstrosity at their front door. This is an extremely powerful source of secret arrows, and their sudden lack of luck will make them putty in your hands. Oh, and you'll have 200 new channels to play with!

3   **Damage their drains**

Some more sabotage is required here. Blocked drains mean a backlog of stagnant chi, so creep around in the dead of night and stuff some dead leaves and other non-suspicious but block-worthy debris down their drains. Then watch their luck flush down the drains. Or, ... whoops! They're blocked! No room for their luck, even!

4   **Wreck their wardrobe – in more ways than one**
Violet can cause depression, so maybe you should slip
some colour dye into your neighbour's washing machine
when they're turning the other way. They will be so
depressed that you won't see them again for weeks.
What a shame.

You can also appeal to their vanity by buying a pretty new mirror as a
present. Insist that they hang it in their hallway, in a position that
directly reflects their front door. That way, you can sweetly claim, they
will always be able to check for lipstick on their teeth or erroneous
grease marks on their shirts. What a fib! In truth, this placement will
ensure that any good chi will zoom straight out of their home, resulting
in a distinct lack of good fortune. The eventual result could even cause
your neighbour to get the urge to move home. Before you know it, they
will have emigrated to Australia. Well done!

## Take total control of your car

Yes, car feng shui really does exist and – surprise, surprise! – it's a hot
new trend in LA, land of the car as well as the here-one-day-gone-the-
next fad. It's actually referred to as 'feng che', which translates literally
as 'wind' and 'vehicle'. And since Los Angeles, with its cloak-and-
dagger movie industry is the kind of place where so much depends on
guarding your own back, feng che must be doing something right.

## The 10 laws of feng che

1   Get a rounded car – in other words, one that deals wonderfully with all that circulating chi. A curvy VW Beetle is perfect.

2   Attach colourful banners to your aerial – these good luck symbols should ensure you never crash.

3   Ditto, a tiny fish tank in your rear window. There are actually cars in LA that have had fish tanks installed.

4   Have no friends? Feel you need to make more? If so, decorate the top of your steering wheel with a floral arrangement.

5   So you're a person who collects enemies like a dog collects fleas? Reposition your rear mirrors so that anyone looking into them sees a reflection. In other words, his own negative chi.

6   Maximize your own good chi by choosing the right roads and avoid crossroads – ooh, all those right angles! Rumour has it that there are now more traffic jams during rush hour on certain crossroad-less routes in LA.

7   Pump up the air conditioning and drive with the windows closed or you will be losing lots of chi.

8   Get rid of vulgar mascots like your favourite nodding dog and any lewd bumper stickers. Replace them with tried-and-tested good luck symbols like the three-legged toad.

9   Always have CDs in the player; otherwise, the chi will escape – it's continually looking for any means possible for an exit.

10  Finally, never park in the corner of a car park because this is a place where there will be too much stagnant chi. Keep on circling until somewhere more auspicious turns up. Hey, no one ever said feng shui would be easy – but it can be nasty.